Maybe Tomorrow I'll Have a Good Time

by Mary Soderstrom

illustrated by Charlotte Epstein Wein

HUMAN SCIENCES PRESS
72 FIFTH AVENUE,
NEW YORK, N.Y. 10011 (212)243-6000

For Elin, with much love

Printed in the United States.

Soderstrom, Mary, 1942-
    Maybe tomorrow I'll have a good time.

    SUMMARY: Marsha Lou is mad and sad during her
first day at the day care center, but thinks maybe she'll
have a good time the next day.
    [1. Day care centers—Fiction] I. Wein, Charlotte
Epstein. II. Title.
PZ7.S68526May   [E]   80-25357
ISBN 0-89885-012-6

Marsha Lou liked having her Mother stay at home to take care of her. Ever since she was a baby her Mother had been there to help her, to do things with her and to wake her up with a hug, a kiss, and a tickle.

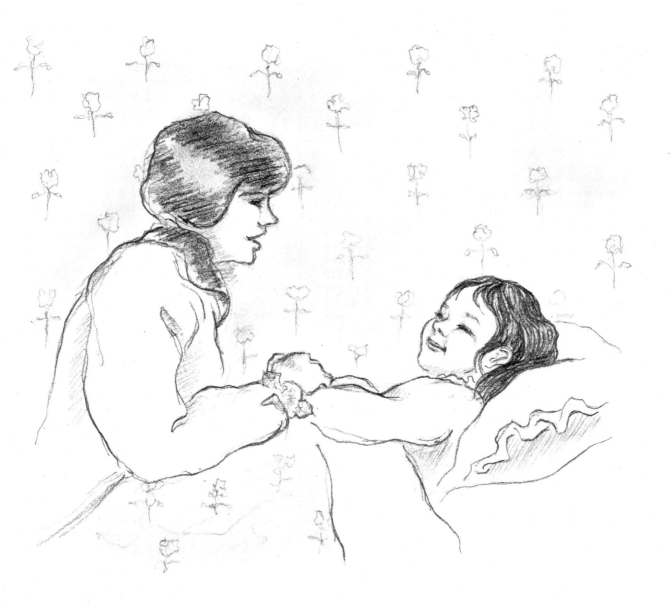

But one day Mother decided it was time to go out to work again. She sat down at the kitchen table where Marsha Lou was drawing and started to explain what was going to happen.

"While I'm working there won't be anyone home to take care of you," she said. "So you'll go to a day care center where some nice people look after children."

Marsha Lou stopped drawing
and looked at her Mother.

"You'll have fun there, you'll really have a good time," Mother went on. "There will be a lot of boys and girls to play with, and things to do. Doesn't that sound like fun?" she asked.

Marsha Lou stared at her a moment. Then she blinked her eyes quickly, almost as if she were going to cry.

"Doesn't it sound nice?" Mother asked again.

Marsha Lou stared for a moment longer.
   Then she nodded,
         but she didn't say yes and she didn't say no.

There were a lot of things to get ready. They had to buy a laundry marking pen, and a lunch box with a Thermos bottle. Then Mother wrote Marsha Lou's name on her jackets, sweaters and mittens, and on a piece of masking tape she stuck to the lunch box.

The night before they made peanut butter sandwiches to put in the lunch box. Marsha Lou got to use the knife to spread the peanut butter, and she washed an apple off under the kitchen faucet with only a little help. Then they put the sandwich, the apple, a container of peach yogurt, and the Thermos filled with milk in the lunch box and put the lunch box in the refrigerator so it would be ready in the morning.

"What a big girl you are," her Mother said as she closed the refrigerator door. "Big enough to make a sandwich almost all by herself. Big enough to have a very good time at the day care center tomorrow. Right?"

Marsha Lou nodded.

But she didn't say yes and she

almost said no.

The next morning they caught a bus at a corner two blocks away. There weren't seats for both of them so Marsha Lou sat on Mother's lap while they looked out the window and Mother talked about what they saw.

"Every morning we'll take this bus," she said, "And go by that building and that park, and get off at this bus stop, and walk down this street. Exciting, isn't it?"

Marsha Lou didn't say yes and she didn't say no. She didn't say anything, not even when they arrived at the day care center and started up the front steps. All she did was hold tightly on to Mother's hand.

Inside a woman with a big smile met them. She was the day care teacher.

"Good morning," she said. "It will be nice to have Marsha Lou with us."

Behind her Marsha Lou could see two girls sitting at a table playing with plasticine. Someone was singing "Ring Around the Rosie," and someone else was yelling "You can't catch me." There were pictures children had drawn on the walls and blue mats for doing somersaults on the floor.

The teacher took Marsha Lou's lunch box from her and led her by the hand to the place where the children hung their coats. As she did, she talked about the things Marsha Lou was going to do. Mother listened and said, "How exciting," once or twice, but finally she knelt down and put her arms around Marsha Lou.

"Okay, sweetie," she said. "I have to go to work now. You be a good girl and have a good time. All right?" Then she stood up quickly. "Good-bye," she said to the teacher.

"Good-bye," the woman said. "Do you want to paint now?" she asked Marsha Lou. "I was just going to get out the painting things when you came in."

Marsha Lou didn't say yes and she didn't say no. She didn't even nod. Instead she took a long look at her Mother walking out the door and she started to cry.

"Mommy," Marsha Lou screamed. Where was she going? When was she going to come back?

"She's just going to work," the teacher said. "She'll be back as soon as she can."

Marsha Lou paid no attention. "I want my Mommy," she wailed.

"She'll be back," the teacher repeated. "Now, would you like to paint?"

"No," Marsha Lou said, and she started to cry again. She cried so hard in fact that she couldn't say all the things she wanted to, like: It wasn't fair, it wasn't nice; it was mean of her Mother to leave her this way.

For a while the woman held her. Then she said, "The other children are waiting for me to get the painting things. If you don't want to paint maybe you can sit here for a while and watch. I'll come back in a minute." As she spoke she set Marsha Lou in a chair at a little table. Marsha Lou tried to hold on for a moment, but finally she let go and sat watching the other children.

The others painted. Then they had milk and crackers with cheese. Then they went outside to play on the swings and the slides. Each time they began something new, the teacher and some of the children came over to ask Marsha Lou if she wanted to join them. Each time she didn't say yes and she didn't say no. She just sat there pretending she didn't see them.

When lunch time came, she ate only because the teacher got her lunch box and led her over to where the others sat eating their lunches. And at nap time, she tried not to listen to the story another teacher told before the others snuggled down to sleep. Instead she thought about how her Mother used to wake her up from her nap with a hug, a kiss, and a tickle.

It was a long afternoon. Marsha Lou watched while other children played with blocks and the doll house, and listened while they sang about Old MacDonald and his farm.

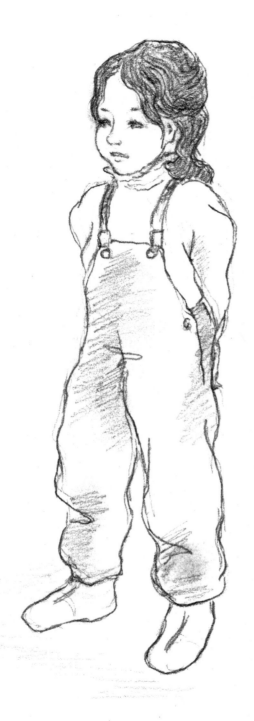

And finally, just when Marsha Lou was wondering
what everyone was going to do next, her Mother walked in.

"Mommy, Mommy," Marsha Lou screamed and came running over.

Mother picked her up and swung her around. "Did you have a good time?" she asked when she'd finished hugging her.

"No," Marsha Lou said, and for a moment she thought she was going to cry again. "I was mad and I was sad."

"You were?" Mother asked, leading her over to where her coat was hanging. "With all the toys and the painting and the things to do? It sure looks like the other children are having a good time."

Marsha Lou turned so she could watch the others while her Mother buttoned up her coat. They were pretending they were elephants now, galumphing around, swinging their arms like trunks. It did look like they were having fun. In fact it looked like they'd been having fun all day.

"I was mad and I was sad," Marsha Lou repeated. Then she reached out and put her arms around her Mother's neck. She pushed her face into her Mother's hair and breathed in the sweet smell, half of flowers, half of Mother. She put her mouth very close to her Mother's ear and she whispered;

"I was mad and I was sad. But maybe ... maybe I'll have a good time tomorrow."

And you know what? She did.

■ Human Sciences Press Children's Books

Arnstein, Helene
BILLY AND OUR NEW BABY
Illustrated by M. Jane Smyth
0-87705-093-7 $9.95   1973
Ages 4 to 8

Barrett, John M.
DANIEL DISCOVERS DANIEL
Pictures by Joe Servello
0-87705-423-1 $9.95   1979
Ages 5 to 10

NO TIME FOR ME
Illustrated by Joe Servello
0-87705-385-5 $9.95   1979
Ages 4 to 8

OSCAR THE SELFISH OCTOPUS
Pictures by Joseph Servello
0-87705-335-9 $9.95   1978
Ages 4 to 8

Beaudry, Jo, and Lynne Ketchum
CASEY GOES TO COURT
Illustrated with photographs by Jack Hamilton
0-89885-088-6 $9.95   1982/June

Berger, Terry
I HAVE FEELINGS
Illustrated with photographs by I. Howard Spivak
0-87705-021-X $9.95   1971
Ages 4 to 8

I HAVE FEELINGS TOO
Illustrated with photographs by Michael Ach
0-87705-441-X $9.95   1979
Ages 4 to 8

Bergstrom, Corinne
LOSING YOUR BEST FRIEND
Illustrated by Patricia Rosàmilia
0-87705-471-1 $9.95   1980
Ages 4 to 8

Berman, Linda
THE GOODBYE PAINTING
Illustrated by Mark Hannon
0-89885-074-6 $9.95   1982/June

Blue, Rose
ME AND EINSTEIN
Illustrated by Peggy Luks
0-87705-388-X $9.95   1979
Ages 8 and up

WISHFUL LYING
Illustrated by Laura Hartman
0-87705-473-8 $9.95   1980
Ages 4 to 8

Boyd, Selma and Pauline Boyd
THE HOW
Making the Best of a Mistake
Illustrated by Peggy Luks
0-87705-176-3 $9.95   1981/April
Ages 4 to 8

Fassler, Joan, Ph.D.
ALL ALONE WITH DADDY
Illustrated by Dorothy Lake Gregory
Revised Edition
0-87705-009-0 $9.95   1971
Ages 4 to 8

BOY WITH A PROBLEM
Illustrated by Stewart Kranz
0-87705-054-6 $9.95   1971
Ages 4 to 8

DON'T WORRY DEAR
Illustrated by Stewart Kranz
0-87705-055-4 $9.95   1969
Ages 4 to 8

THE MAN OF THE HOUSE
Illustrated by Peter Landa
Revised Edition
0-87705-010-4 $9.95   1969
Ages 4 to 8

MY GRANDPA DIED TODAY
Illustrated by Stewart Kranz
0-87705-053-8 $9.95   1971
Ages 4 to 8

ONE LITTLE GIRL
Illustrated by M. Jane Smyth
0-87705-008-2 $9.95   1969

Fink, Dale Borman
MR. SILVER AND MRS. GOLD
Illustrated by Shirley Chan
0-87705-447-9 $9.95   1980
Ages 4 to 8

Gatch, Jean
SCHOOL MAKES SENSE... SOMETIMES
Illustrated by Susan Turnbull
0-87705-494-0 $9.95   1980
Ages 4 to 10

Gold, Phyllis
PLEASE DON'T SAY HELLO
Illustrated with Photographs by Carl Baker
0-87705-211-5 $9.95   1975
Ages 6 to 10

Goldsmith, Howard
TOTO THE TIMID TURTLE
Illustrated by Shirley Chan
0-87705-524-4 $9.95   1981
Ages 4 to 8

Green, Phyllis
A NEW MOTHER FOR MARTHA
Illustrated by Peggy Luks
087705-330-8 $9.95   1978
Ages 4 to 8

Greenberg, Polly
I KNOW I'M MYSELF BECAUSE...
Illustrated by Jennifer Barrett
0-89885-045-2 $9.95   1981/July
Ages 2 to 6

Greene, Laura
CHANGE
Getting to Know about Ebb and Flow
Illustrated by Gretchen Mayo
087705-401-0 $9.95   1981/April
Ages 4 to 8

HELP
Getting to Know about Needing and Giving
Illustrated by Gretchen Mayo
087705-402-9 $9.95   1981/April
Ages 4 to 8

Hazen, Barbara Shook
IT'S A SHAME ABOUT THE RAIN
Illustrated by Bernadette Simmons
0-89885-050-9 $9.95   1982/January

IF IT WEREN'T FOR BENJAMIN
(I'd Always Get to Lick the Icing Spoon)
Illustrated by Laura Hartman
0-87705-384-7 $9.95   1977
Ages 4 to 8

TWO HOMES TO LIVE IN
A Child's-Eye View of Divorce
Illustrated by Peggy Luks
087705-313-8 $9.95   1977
Ages 4 to 8

VERY SHY
Illustrated by Sue Rotella
0-89885-067-3 $9.95   1982/January

Horner, Althea J.
LITTLE BIG GIRL
Illustrated by Patricia C. Rosamilia
0-89885-098-3 $9.95   1982/June

"I and the Others" Writer's Collective
IT'S SCARY SOMETIMES
Illustrated by the children themselves
0-87705-366-9 $9.95   1978
Ages 4 to 8

Jacobson, Jane
CITY, SING FOR ME
A Country Child Moves to the City
Illustrated by Amy Rowen
0-87705-358-8 $9.95   1978
Ages 6 to 10

Leggett, Linda and Linda Andrews
THE ROSE-COLORED GLASSES
Melanie Adjusts to Poor Vision
Illustrated by Laura Hartman
087705-408-8 $9.95   1979
Ages 8 and up

Levine, Edna S., Ph.D., Litt.D.
LISA AND HER SOUNDLESS WORLD
Illustrated by Gloria Kamen

A Children's Book of the Year, 1974, Award Granted by the Children's Book Committee of the Child Study Association of America.

0-87705-104-6 $9.95   1974

Menzel, Barbara
WOULD YOU RATHER?
Illustrated by Sumishta Brahm
0-89885-076-2 $9.95   1982/January

Rappaport, Doreen, Susan Kempler and Michele Spirn
A MAN CAN BE . . .
Illustrated with photographs by Russell Dian
0-89885-046-0 $9.95   1981/July
Ages 2-6

Rappaport, Doreen
BUT SHE'S STILL MY GRANDMA
Illustrated by Bernadette Simmons
0-89885-072-X $9.95   1982/January

Sheehan, Cilla, M.A.C.P.
THE COLORS THAT I AM
Illustrated by Glen Elliot
089885-047-0 $10.95   1981/July
Ages 4 to 10

Soderstrom, Mary
MAYBE TOMORROW I'LL HAVE A GOOD TIME
Illustrated by Charlotte Epstein Wein
0-89885-012-6 $9.95   1981/July

Stefanik, Alfred T.
COPYCAT SAM
Illustrated by Laura Huff
0-89885-058-4 $9.95   1982/January

Strauss, Joyce
HOW DOES IT FEEL . . .
Illustrated by Sumishta Brahm
0-89885-048-7 $9.95   1981/July
Ages 4 to 8

Wittels, Harriet and Joan Greisman
THINGS I HATE
Illustrated by Jerry McConnel
0-87705-096-1 $9.95   1973
Ages 4 to 8

Complete Children's Catalog available upon request

JUDITH CASELEY

The Cousins

Greenwillow Books, New York

Watercolor paints and colored pencils
were used for the full-color art.
The text type is ITC Esprit.

Library of Congress Cataloging-in-Publication Data
Caseley, Judith.
Jenny and Jessica / Judith Caseley.
p.   cm.
Summary: As first cousins grow, their parents learn how
very different Jenny and Jessica are from each other.
ISBN 0-688-08433-8   ISBN 0-688-08434-6 (lib. bdg.)
[1. Cousins — Fiction.]   I. Title.
PZ7.C2677Jen 1990
[E] — dc19   88-34903   CIP   AC

To the original first cousins,
Jenna and Jessica

Jenny and Jessica were first cousins. They didn't look a
bit alike.

"Night and day," said Jenny's mama. "As opposite as can be."

"Chalk and cheese," said Grandma. "You wouldn't know
their mothers were sisters."

Jenny was born with lots of black hair.
"She takes after my side of the family," said
Jenny's papa.
"Nonsense," said Grandma. "She looks just
like my sister Bertha."

Jessica was born with one blond curl.

"Our little princess," said Jessica's papa.

"She looks just like me," said Jessica's mama.

"She's bald," said Grandma, "like her grandpa was."

Jenny crawled for the longest while.
"Will she ever walk?" asked her mama.
"Babies take their own sweet time," said the doctor.
"I'd like her to be good in gym," said Jenny's mama.
"I was," said Grandma. "She will be, too."

Jessica climbed before she could walk.
"I found her halfway up the rose trellis," said her mama.
"You can't stop watching for a minute," said Grandma.

Jenny liked to fingerpaint. Mama put on her smock and
spread newspaper on the floor.
"My little artist," said Papa, and he hung Jenny's pictures
on the refrigerator door.

Jessica liked to empty drawers and throw her toys
in the trash basket. She liked to build block houses
and knock them down.
"All that energy!" said Papa.
"I'm exhausted," said Mama.

On Jenny's third birthday, Grandma gave her a toy piano.
"Play us a tune," said Grandma.
Jenny shook her head.
Mama took Jenny's hands and helped her play a little song.
Jessica danced in time to the music.
Jenny pulled her hands away.
"No," she said, and she drew a picture instead.

"They're nothing alike," said Jenny's mama.
"Night and day," said Jessica's papa.
"Chalk and cheese," said Grandma.

On Jessica's third birthday, Grandma gave her
a big red bird that talked.
Jessica tried to make it dance instead.
It wouldn't. So Jessica put it in the closet and
shut the door.
"Oh dear," said Grandma. "They don't sell birds
that dance."

Jenny took the bird out and painted a picture of it.
"She doesn't take after me," said Papa.
"Me, either," said Mama. "I can't draw a straight line."
"She gets it from Grandpa," said Grandma. "He had
  beautiful handwriting."

When they were six, Jenny and Jessica took ballet
lessons together.
"Jessica loves it," said her mama.
"Jenny doesn't mention it," said her papa.

The next time Jenny came home from ballet class,
she painted a picture.
"What a nice painting," said Mama. "What is it?"
"It's a little girl dancing," said Jenny.
"Why does she look so sad?" asked Mama.
"Her feet hurt," said Jenny.

Jenny and Jessica went to an arts-and-crafts class.
They made pictures with feathers and glitter and paint.
They made baskets and bright paper flowers.
"Isn't this fun?" said Jenny.
"No," said Jessica.

Jessica took her basket home.

She leaped into the air and handed Mama a flower.

"How pretty," said Mama. "Do you like your class?"

Jessica did a pirouette. "It reminds me of the dentist," she said.

One day Jenny and Jessica and their mamas took a
walk to the library.
They passed the dancing school. Jenny held her nose.
"Jenny is leaving dance class," said her mama.
"She likes to paint better."

They passed the community center. Jessica covered her
eyes so she wouldn't see it.

"Jessica doesn't want to go to the arts-and-crafts class
anymore," said her mama. "It reminds her of the dentist."

"They have nothing in common," said both mamas.

"Chalk and cheese," said Jenny's mama. "Night and day."

They passed the fruit market.

There was a big sign in the window:

"Try Granny Smith apples — They're one of a kind!"

"Just like me," said Jessica.

"Just like me," said Jenny.

"One of a kind!" they shouted.

Their mothers smiled at each other.

"Smart as whips," said Jessica's mama.

"Bright as buttons," said Jenny's mama.

"Two peas in a pod!"

Then one first cousin took the other's hand,
and one sister took the other's arm,
and they all went into the library together.